Sticky
Vickie

First published in 2008 by
Franklin Watts
338 Euston Road
London
NW1 3BH

Franklin Watts Australia
Level 17/207 Kent Street
Sydney
NSW 2000

A CIP catalogue record for this book is available
from the British Library.

ISBN 978 0 7496 7978 1 (hbk)
ISBN 978 0 7496 7986 6 (pbk)

Series Editor: Jackie Hamley
Series Advisor: Dr Barrie Wade
Series Designer: Peter Scoulding

Printed in China

Franklin Watts is a division of
Hachette Children's Books,
an Hachette Livre UK company.

Sticky Vickie

by Enid Richemont

Illustrated by Gwyneth Williamson

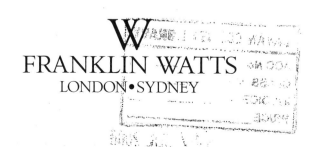

FRANKLIN WATTS
LONDON • SYDNEY

The prince wanted a wife.

He told everyone in the country, "I will only marry someone who makes me laugh."

Vickie went to the
wise witch to see if
she knew any jokes.

"I have brought you a present," said Vickie. "It's a walking stick."

"Thank you. Here's a sticky present for you!" said the wise witch.

"Now go and see the prince!"

Vickie put the present in her bag and set off.

"I'll have that bag!" growled a thief.

But when the thief
grabbed the bag,
his hands got stuck.

A goose nipped the thief.
Her beak stuck to him.

"I'll catch that goose!"
cried the farmer.

He got stuck to her.

His dog leapt up and
stuck to his trousers.

"Come back!" called
the farmer's wife.

She got stuck to the dog.

At the palace, a princess joked, "Knock! Knock!"

But the prince just yawned.

Then Vickie walked in with the thief, the goose, the farmer, the dog and the farmer's wife all stuck behind her.

The prince giggled.

Then he laughed.

28

Then he roared!

Vickie and the prince were married, and they have stuck together ever since!

31

Leapfrog has been specially designed to fit the requirements of the National Literacy Framework. It offers real books for beginning readers by top authors and illustrators. There are 26 Leapfrog stories to choose from:

Look out for Leapfrog

FAIRY TALES

Rhyming stories are available with Leapfrog Rhyme Time.